Halloween Rescue!

by Cynthia Stierle

illustrated by Artful Doodl

Based on the TV series *Go, Diego, Go!*™ as seen on Ni

SIMON SPOTLIGHT
An imprint of Simon & Schuster Children's Publishing Division
1230 Avenue of the Americas, New York, New York 10020
© 2007 Viacom International Inc. All rights reserved. NICK JR., *Go, Diego, Go!*, and all related titles,
logos, and characters are trademarks of Viacom International Inc.
All rights reserved, including the right of reproduction in whole or in part in any form.
SIMON SPOTLIGHT and colophon are registered trademarks of Simon & Schuster, Inc.
Manufactured in the United States of America
First Edition 10 9 8 7 6 5 4 3 2 1
ISBN-13: 978-1-4169-3351-9
ISBN-10: 1-4169-3351-4

D1275532

¡Hola! I'm Diego. Baby Jaguar and I are getting ready for Halloween. I'm dressed like Baby Jaguar! *Mreow, mreow!* And Baby Jaguar is dressed as me! Ha ha!

Chreeep-chreeep-chreeep!
Oh, no! That sounds like an animal in trouble. It may be Halloween, but we're still Animal Rescuers! Let's get to the Animal Rescue Center and figure out who needs our help!

We need to ask Click to help us find the animal in trouble. Say "Click!"

Look! Click is showing us a picture of a free-tail bat. It's nighttime, so it's time for the free-tail bats to wake up and play. Bats sleep during the day and come out at night. But I don't see any other bats in the picture. Where are the bat's friends?

Look! That bat is flying over a pile of rocks that fell down the mountain and blocked in a cave. The bat's friends must be trapped inside!

We have to move the rocks so the other bats can get out of the cave for Halloween night. Come on, Baby Jaguar. *¡Al rescate!* To the rescue!

Lead the way, Baby Jaguar! Jaguars can see well in the dark. I'll need my flashlight so that I can see like Baby Jaguar . . . and like all the other animals that come out at night!

Look, it's a rare black jaguar. His fur looks as black as the night sky, but he actually has spots just like Baby Jaguar.

Happy Halloween, *Señor* Jaguar!

We have to keep going down this path to get to the bat, but look! An orb spider has built its web across the path.

We don't want to damage the web—the spider needs it to catch food. How can we get past the web?

Great thinking, Baby Jaguar! Let's crawl under the web. *¡Gatea, gatea!* Crawl, crawl!

We're getting closer to the bat's cave. But Baby Jaguar has stopped again. What is it, Baby Jaguar? Oh! There's a big gorge ahead of us. How can we get to the other side of the gorge quickly?

Look! Baby Jaguar is using a tree that fell over the gorge as a bridge. Jaguars have great balance. I'll have to hold out my arms so that I can balance as well as him.

We made it to the mountain. I see the pile of rocks blocking the cave! Do you see the bat? You have to look carefully. Try to see in the night like a jaguar. Good finding! There's the bat now!

Let's move these rocks so we can rescue the bats trapped in the cave. Let's count as we move the rocks! *¡Uno! ¡Dos! ¡Tres! ¡Cuatro! ¡Cinco!*

Whew! That's five rocks, but there are still a lot of rocks left. If we only move one rock at a time, the bats will miss Halloween. Who can we ask for help?

Rescue Pack can help us. He can transform into anything we need. To activate my Rescue Pack, say "¡Actívate!"
What can Rescue Pack turn into to help us move the rocks?

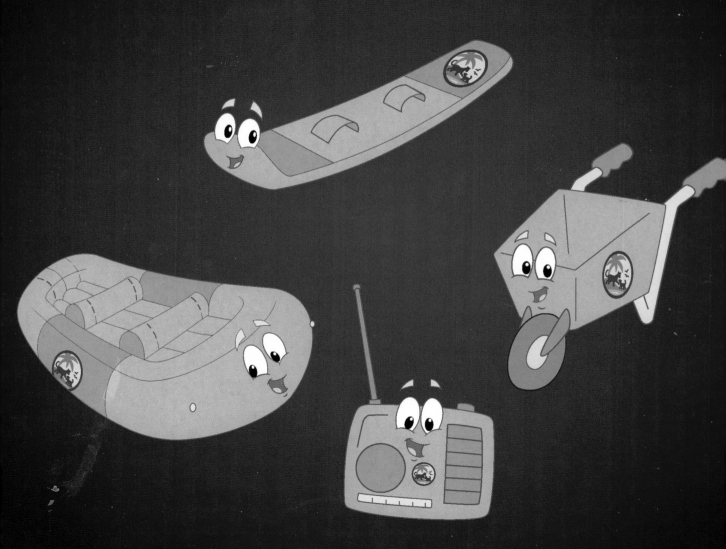

Great! A wheelbarrow is just what we need! We can put lots of rocks in the wheelbarrow and move them away quickly.
Let's get to work!

¡Misión cumplida! Rescue complete! The bats are free. Look at them flying out to enjoy Halloween night!

Thanks for leading the way tonight, Baby Jaguar. I'm glad jaguars are so good at moving and seeing in the dark.
Happy Halloween!